FLOWERS OF WAR

Flowers of War

by

Mark Howard Jones

Black Shuck Books
www.BlackShuckBooks.co.uk

First published in the UK by Black Shuck Books, 2019

978-1-913038-39-7

With thanks to:

Steve J. Shaw for allowing me to let slip the dogs of war.

S. T. Joshi for his support and wise words.

John and Kate, for their encouragement and for just being themselves.

Fred and Pickle, the household gods.

And, most important of all, to Alice, without whom nothing would be possible.

Travelling Across the City in Autumn

A moth fluttered through the darkness, nudging again and again at the glass inside which the candle burned. A lost stranger in the chill of the night, thinking it had found home.

The girl peered closely at the night visitor, wishing there was a way she could talk to it. Its dark wings kept up their futile flapping. She felt like helping it... but helping it to do what? if it got to its goal it would be devoured by the flame.

"Silly thing," she whispered to it. She turned at the sound behind her to see her father enter the room.

He caught sight of the candle in the jar and took two large steps across to where she sat. He grabbed the jar from the window sill and placed it on a small table on the far side of the room.

Light swung around the room, shadows

dancing up the walls and across the ceiling, as the candle moved. The moth fluttered in circles, then flew away into the darkness, seeking a new illusion of home.

"Sweetheart, you've got to keep the candle away from the window. There might still be soldiers down in the city. We don't want them to know we're here, do we?"

The girl's dark eyes searched the floor. "But you said it was all right."

He picked her up and carried her to the almost undamaged sofa. Setting her down, he sat next to her. 'That was in summer, when there were plenty of leaves on the trees," he said, gently. "Look out of the window now."

The window had a single broken pane of glass left at one side of the frame. Obediently the girl raised her eyes and saw black, bare branches against a darkening sky in which stars had reluctantly begun to appear. She nodded.

"Now the leaves have started to fall from the trees, anyone who looks up can see the light easily."

As if to underline his remarks, he picked up the piece of flat wood that served as a shutter and secured it over the window for the night.

He'd chosen the farmhouse because it had a good view of the city below. If anything moved down there, they'd have plenty of warning and could get out before any trouble arrived.

The abandoned farm had been their home for over a month. Tarpaulins shielded them from the worst of the weather. He'd set up his daughter's bedroom in the least damaged part of the building, so she'd be safer than if she was taking her chances elsewhere in the half-ruined structure.

His experienced eye told him that the house had probably been hit on one side by a tank shell, taking off part of the roof and destroying most of the end wall.

Relics of the former inhabitants lay everywhere, but they left them where they were for fear of raising any ghosts.

~

The moon was high and almost perfectly round. It hung above the city and shone revealingly down.

Most of the taller buildings had been demolished by the fighting, but here and there one or two remained, like broken teeth in a ragged mouth.

From his lofty vantage point, he saw the odd fire glowing here or there inside the ruined buildings. People were still trying to live in the city, and a fire at night was safer because smoke was much less visible in the dark. But predators were on the prowl at night, too.

Shrugging off the cold, he turned and headed across the small paved yard to the house. Bed was waiting but, even though he felt exhausted, he wasn't looking forward to it.

He knew that sleep was the only honest state humanity ever experienced. The only time when they were unable to lie, cheat, deceive themselves or manoeuvre for some imagined advantage.

Yet it was also when they were at their most physically fragile, able to be taken advantage of by even the weakest waking individual.

He feared both equally, and always slept as if his bed was ablaze.

~

"How do you want your porridge – soupy or gloopy?" He always asked her the same question.

Her answer was always the same but it was another part of the game that he tried to make her life into.

She giggled. "Gloopy, daddy."

He dished out a bowl of porridge. It was as thick as he could make it, given their dwindling supplies. They both began spooning it into their mouths.

"Mummy came to see me again last night, daddy."

He sighed softly to himself. "But you never met your mother, Mari. She died when you were born. So you can't really know what she looks like, can you?"

Mari looked sulky. "It was her."

"Well, I sleep nearby and I didn't hear her come in, Mari."

"But you were snoring again, daddy," she said, in a tone that reminded him of her mother.

He sighed and nodded. "Believe me, they're just dreams. They must be." He felt aggrieved having to explain things to her. He'd been trained to have a strict military mind, not to pander to the fantasies of a small girl, even if she was his daughter.

"They're not dreams, daddy. I know they're not. I've seen her. She's waiting ..."

He looked into her dark, serious eyes. She often talked as if she was much older than her seven years. Perhaps it was because she'd seen and suffered much more than a child of her age should.

Sometimes he had to stop and remind himself of her age when he was explaining things to her – then he'd backtrack, using simpler language and less complicated ideas.

"She said she wants to help me," Mari persisted.

"But how can..." He stopped, feeling outflanked. He had to justify it to himself somehow, so he told himself he thought it only right that Mari should visit her mother's grave, even if it was just once. No matter how much distress it might cause him.

He gazed down into the empty bowl before him. "All right. All right. I've got some things to do today, but we'll go tomorrow."

She tried to smile at him as best she could.

~

Sitting alone on his bed, he slipped the photograph of his wife from his worn leather wallet. He held it up, the candlelight revealing her dark eyes and a smile that he would die to see just once more.

He remembered her being more beautiful than she was in the photograph. Perhaps women always seemed more beautiful when they were alive in front of you, instead of frozen in a photograph, or locked in the past, or just held in your heart.

Sometimes her absent voice, smooth as peach skin, filled his head from ear to ear, echoing behind his eyes. It whispered admonition or praise for the way he was neglecting or caring for the daughter she'd unwillingly left in his care. Her constant monologue made him a better father, he felt sure. Never allowed to forget his duties, he strove to be better each day. Each day, long and lonely.

He saw her in their daughter's face but she was not there, not really.

Frequently in those days he found himself lulled into an uneasy sleep by a dead woman's prayers.

~

The sky was bright and clear on the morning they were to set off. High above, a silver line drawn across the blue by an airliner reminded him that, somewhere else, life was carrying on as normal.

He buried their essential supplies – their last matches, two oil lamps and a large can of fuel – under a bush, and then covered over the fresh earth with dead twigs and fallen leaves. It was unlikely that anyone would stumble upon the farmhouse when they were away, hidden as it was from the road. But if they did, he wanted to be sure they found nothing worth looting.

By the time he'd finished his work, the sky had clouded over. A bank of dark grey clouds threatened to release its rain at any second. He headed for the house.

Before he'd even made the dozen yards back, the rain had begun to fall in large drops. He noticed a pattern form on the cracked paving stone at his feet.

The rain spatters reminded him of a shrapnel pattern he'd seen years ago. The one that had broken his daughter and murdered his wife.

She'd been at the market when a suicide bomber blew himself up just yards from her. She'd been eight months pregnant.

He remembers rushing to the hospital only to be confronted by the surgeon, leaving the operating theatre. His wife would never leave.

"The child is still alive." The doctor took him to a room and showed him an X-ray of his wife, cut open by shrapnel and splinters of someone else's bones. And there, in an image that made her look like a ghost, was the injured baby living inside her.

The child is still alive. But there is so little of her.

He remembered seeing her for the first time in intensive care, so small and frail, and his feelings tore him in pieces. Once the storm had subsided, nearly a day later, he realised what an enormous task lay ahead of him.

~

Wheelchairs were in desperately short supply in a city half eaten by conflict. But an army doctor friend of his had adapted an old Bergen rucksack so that he could carry his daughter on his back. The addition of a couple of sturdy leather straps around his chest and waist made sure she was always secure.

She delighted in the device, of course, and

had even twisted it so she could see over his left shoulder while being carried.

In any case, Mari was very light for a girl of her age. She was no challenge at all for a soldier used to carrying a full pack and rifle.

~

They set off through the woodland that hid the farm from the road, wet leaves being kicked up by his heavy boots. He had walked a quarter of a mile when the road appeared through the trees.

It was just an ordinary two-lane road, bordered by trees on either side. Hardly any traffic used it now. Only occasional abandoned vehicles betrayed the fact that things were not as they had been.

He rounded a bend in the road, past the rusting wreck of a burnt-out car, and stopped in his tracks.

To one side, almost hidden in the shade of a large conifer, was an armoured vehicle. He recognised the type from his service – it was one that had been used by both sides. It could carry a maximum of six people, but that was six too many, whatever their allegiance.

He retraced his steps and crouched down

behind the wrecked car. "I'll just leave you here a few minutes, sweetheart," he told Mari, unbuckling the harness. "I'm going to take a look. You'll be safer here."

She nodded and helped him to free himself from the carrying harness. She lay on her side in the pine needles that filled up the ditch, hidden by the old car.

He approached the vehicle with caution. He'd hoped this would be a day without surprises, but realised that was forlorn. Any markings on the vehicle to tell him who might be driving it had been obscured by mud.

It hadn't been there when he'd passed this way three days ago, but it appeared abandoned. One of the heavy armoured doors was hanging open.

He'd ridden in the big four-wheeled vehicles himself during the war. And he'd seen comrades die in them when they had blown apart after being hit by an incendiary round.

Cautiously, he crept around to the open door of the vehicle. Struggling to make sure his boots made as little sound as possible on the road – not easy for a big man – he prepared to throw himself flat if a gun barrel suddenly pointed his way.

Both front seats were empty. He breathed a sigh of relief and continued to creep towards the vehicle. The rear compartment might hold someone, alive or dead.

He put his hand on the door gently and moved it so that the side mirror gave a view of the inside. It seemed to be empty. Just to be sure he banged on the side of the vehicle hard and yelled, waiting for any sound of movement. When none came, he clambered onto the front seat and had a good look around. There was a blood stain on the floor but whoever had been driving had left nothing useful behind.

Satisfied the vehicle was safe, he returned to get Mari. "It's OK, sweetheart. It's safe. We can save a lot of time by driving into the city."

He lifted her up and carried her across to the vehicle, carefully buckling the safety harness into place once she was sitting inside.

Slamming the heavy door behind him, he pressed the starter button and the powerful engine growled at him, like an animal angry at being awakened from a comfortable slumber. He eased through the gears until it began to purr instead.

"Here we go," he said and released the brake.

Immediately the great metal beast began to lurch forward unevenly. Clearly there was something wrong with the engine. That explains why it was abandoned, he thought. He slipped it into the lowest gear and the thing moved forward slowly, reluctantly. At least it was all downhill.

He smiled down at his daughter, who looked worried. "It's a bit happier now, isn't it?" She nodded, seeming relieved.

They rode down the hill for a mile or so before the road began to level off and a change of gear was called for. The gearbox fought back and an awful grinding noise came from the guts of the heavy steel monster.

He switched off the engine and wrestled the thing out of gear so that they could freewheel for as long as possible. When they were almost at a halt he started it up again. This time the engine didn't complain so much, but he was careful to drive slowly now that they were on the flat road.

The trees had thinned out by this point, and the skeleton of the city came into view. To one side of the road was a retail park. It had been badly shelled, and the buildings were now hollowed out boxes filled with blackened timbers. The unstable walls framed twisted metal girders that were rapidly rusting.

The engine began to make an alarming noise. The last thing he wanted to do was draw attention to them. He scanned the road ahead constantly as he eased back on what little acceleration they still had and let the vehicle freewheel again.

A large road sign read 'Welcome to Pelu'. Underneath someone had attempted to repair the broken sign with some 'helpful' advice. It had been changed from 'Please Drive Carefully' to 'Please Drink Your Own Piss – There's No Water!'.

He chuckled inwardly and was glad they'd brought three water bottles and a full canteen. That should be more than enough for their hopefully brief trip.

"Yuuch!"

His daughter's vocal disgust at the sign prompted him to be serious for a second. "Ignore that silly sign. We've got plenty of water with us. Don't worry."

He tried to coax the engine back to life again. It complained once or twice, roared into life and then purred angrily. It was short lived.

Just as the engine gave up altogether, he saw that the road ahead was flooded. So much for 'no water', he thought.

The vehicle rolled slowly to a halt and he put the brake on. Climbing out, he walked down the slight incline in the road to the edge of the water. Perhaps a main had burst or the nearby river had burst its banks. Or maybe both.

He found a broken brick and tossed it into the slowly moving water. It plopped noisily in, revealing that the water was only a foot or so deep. It was about 12 to 15 feet wide.

He climbed back into the vehicle. "Time to get out, sweetheart. We'll have to wade across some water, OK?"

She nodded. After clambering into her harness, he hoisted her onto his back, slinging the knapsack with their provisions over his other arm. He'd carried heavier loads when he was in the army, but none of them had been this precious.

At the water's edge once more, he stood looking into the rippling surface for a few seconds. "OK. Here we go then!"

The chilly water flooded over the top of his boots and through the lace holes as he took his first step. He began to wade in deeper and found that the submerged surface was slightly slippery.

Five steps in, the water was past his knees and he struggled once or twice to keep his balance. Halfway across, he stopped to re-balance himself.

Nearby the water moved more swiftly, seemingly of its own accord. Then he felt something brush his leg. And another movement followed it.

"Daddy ...?" His daughter sounded scared.

"I know, sweetie. We'll be OK. Don't worry," he lied.

The last thing he wanted to do was drop her – or their supplies – but he needed to get out of the water fast. He had no idea what was in the water. They might just be harmless fish that had swum in from the river. But then again, they might not be.

Several yards away, something green and long broke the surface for a second before seeking submarine refuge once more.

Placing his left foot as firmly on the hard surface as he could, he braced himself carefully. "Hang on, sweetie," he said, grasping his daughter's harness more firmly. Just as he was about to take a large step forward, the water around his right foot began to move swiftly. Something had latched onto his boot.

Using all his strength and spurred on by a sense of urgency, he hauled his right leg out of the water and strode forward. A large, ugly grey-green fish had its teeth sunk into the leather of his old army boot and was flung forward by the impetus of his long stride. The fish flopped onto dry land and began its long ballet of death.

In another two steps he was out of the water, which thrashed with activity behind him.

He walked over to where the fish lay writhing and, placing his boot a decent distance from its mouth, half kicked it back into the water. It was ugly and vicious but that didn't mean it deserved to die.

"It was horrible," said Mari softly. He grunted in reply and turned to look down the road.

~

He had studied a map of the city before they had started out. But the city no longer resembled that map, and he pitied whoever it was that would have the task of drawing a new one.

Entire districts had been flattened or torched, outlying suburbs were no more than graveyards, and the centre was a hollowed-out shell that had been the cruellest of killing grounds.

Somehow they had to negotiate their way across or around these zones of desolation to reach their destination.

They had been walking down the broad road into the city for about 30 minutes. Occasional shots could be heard in the distance – the fighting had stopped, but the firing hadn't.

In truth, during the fighting he had been on no-one's side, despite his uniform. His true allegiance had been to himself and his pregnant wife. In his mind, he was an army of one and he dared trust nobody.

He had sympathy with both those screaming in the streets and those dreaming in the hills. But he also knew that they were both wrong.

An old petrol station advertised prices that were years out of date. A noisy group of sparrows used it as a perch, commenting to each other on the strangers invading their territory.

The crunch of heavy boots on broken glass raised the hairs on the back of his neck. Several soldiers appeared from behind some small factory units next to the petrol station. Immediately one of the men spotted them and he heard rifle bolts being pulled back.

A sergeant pushed to the front of the group and began heading in their direction. Dealing with soldiers of any description was something he'd hoped to avoid, but he relaxed a little when he recognised their insignia.

While he was still some distance away, the sergeant began yelling. "Stay where you are! Don't move!"

He'd had no intention of making so fatal an error. When the sergeant was close enough he threw his own question at the soldiers. "You're with Colonel Nairn, aren't you?"

The sergeant looked at him warily. "Yes."

"You're 5th Tactical Group then. I used to be a Lieutenant in 3rd Troop." It wasn't true. He'd only fought alongside them but any small lie that gained him some purchase with them was acceptable.

"What's left of 'em, yes."

The man's eyes wandered away for a few seconds, lost in memories, before his gaze returned to his guest. "Why aren't you in uniform... Lieutenant?"

He was surprised at the question. Stating the obvious seemed to be the best thing. "Because the war's over. I left the army."

The answer didn't seem to make sense to the sergeant. "You mean you were discharged?"

Sighing inwardly, he continued his simple explanation. "Well, yes. I—"

A buzzing noise that had been growing louder in the background suddenly burst over a ruined rooftop and filled the street.

Looking up, he saw a small, propeller-driven observation plane swoop low before roaring off again. The thing looked several wars out-of-date but was obviously still serviceable.

The sergeant and his men scattered, finding shelter as best they could in the shattered buildings that lay along one side of the street. He watched them disappear into cover before realising he had frozen, and that he should do the same.

His daughter whimpered as he clutched her head, holding it close to his shoulder, and began to run.

Within seconds the plane re-appeared. A small dark shape appeared from the cockpit and plummeted to the ground.

He scrambled through the shattered outline of what used to be a doorway, going down on one knee painfully as he sought the safety of the darkened interior.

The buzzing of the lethal insect began to fade. Somebody swat it, for God's sake! a voice in his head yelled.

There was a loud noise as the grenade exploded, followed by a prolonged yelling. He heard voices raised in controlled panic as gunfire was aimed at where the plane had been a moment before. The firing continued for a few more moments before the sergeant called a halt to it.

"Are you OK, sweetheart?" he mumbled into his daughter's hair. She nodded but kept her face buried in his shoulder.

Arching his neck around the edge of the ruined door frame, he peered out into the open area. Several men were attending to a bleeding comrade while the sergeant motioned his arm to an unseen vehicle.

A shabby-looking truck roared into view and the wounded man was loaded into the back. As the aircraft engine grew louder once more, the sergeant caught his eye and gestured upwards. "Tell *him* the war's over... Sir!"

The sergeant was the last to scramble aboard before the truck roared off, lurching over pieces of rubble and raising a cloud of dust that a blind man could follow.

Dusting himself down, he set off towards what he remembered had been an expensive area to live. Within a few minutes an odd sound began to fill the air, lying somewhere in the sonic no-man's land between the low crackle of fireworks going off and someone stacking chairs noisily.

They rounded a large pile of rubble that had once been an apartment block and saw large black shapes in the distance. He stopped and stepped back into cover.

The things – whatever they were – didn't seem to have spotted them.

There were no markings on them. It was impossible to tell if they were machines or some sort of living thing. If they were alive, he didn't want to think of what sort of broken mind could dream up something like that.

Standing on four legs that extended from high on their bodies, each black thing had a long neck, ending in an indistinct shape that moved back and forth constantly across the ground.

They emitted a sucking or inhaling sound as they went.

He stared, appalled, as the things picked their way over the ground, clicking over the rubble in a serried rank. Now and then one of them stumbled on the loose rubble, only to be pushed back into place by the next in line.

Are there men in those things? he wondered. They behaved more like animals, but surely nature couldn't have made something that wrong.

Towards the end of the war, he'd heard that both sides were working on some pretty strange weapons. Could these things be the result?

He would have been able to smell if any bodies had been left in the rubble. There was nothing.

While the most obvious human remains had been cleared long ago, he presumed this area must still have been rich in detritus. Blood, bone fragments, bits of brain and fragments of fear must have littered the ground or have soaked into the soil. These things were feeding on them, noisily.

He couldn't imagine what they'd want with such fragments. Still they continued diligently in their task.

"Daddy, I'm scared," Mari whispered. There was a small sob in her voice.

He patted her tiny hand where it clung to his coat. He didn't want her to know that he was just as frightened and bewildered as she was.

At least he had his training to fall back on. "It's all right, sweetheart. We'll just go another way, shall we?"

He began to pick his way carefully among the rubble, looking out for any hazards and skirting around overgrown shrubs.

A clattering of stones made him look back. A young boy – not much older than his daughter – had broken cover and was heading away from the things.

Two of them raised their long necks and broke formation to pursue him. They were surprisingly fast for such bulky things, he thought. They'll soon catch him, and God knows what they'll do when they run him down. He couldn't understand how the black things knew where the boy was – they had no eyes or ears as far as he could see. Maybe they were machines, after all.

The boy tried to scramble up a steep bank of rubble, but it was too much for him and he came back down almost immediately. His pursuers were even closer now. The boy, panting heavily, headed towards the place where he and his daughter were hiding, ducking quickly behind an overgrown bush.

No! No! No! Don't bring them this way! screamed a voice in the back of his head. He felt almost ashamed at the thought that, if he only had a gun, he could kill the boy and stop him from endangering them.

He felt equally ashamed, but also relieved, when he saw the leg of the nearest black object reach forward in mid-run and push the boy, causing him to tip forward into a pile of bricks. As the boy lay on his face in the dust his two pursuers towered over him, clicking excitedly.

He didn't know what would happen, and he didn't want to see, so he edged cautiously away from the place.

They had only gone a few steps when the screaming started. He was thankful it didn't last long. But he stopped in his tracks when he heard a sound like bones snapping, and then of something wet hitting a hard surface. He tried to stop his imagination from providing any images to match the sounds.

He forced his feet forward again. He had to get his daughter to safety, quickly. If anywhere *was* safe anymore.

A few more minutes walking brought them to a line of shops that had been left standing. The first three looked as if they might open again any day, after a visit from the glaziers and a lick of paint.

The nearest was a clothing shop. Looters had left a pile of flimsy fashion items scattered across the pavement. They were covered in dust and rubble in a display of disaster chic.

Behind the shattered glass was a jumble of scorched clothing and a half-destroyed mannequin. As they passed by, Mari giggled at something. He turned his head to look at the former fashion outlet.

The mannequin had clearly been struck in the head by a bullet. It looked as if the smile was exploding off her face. Mari stretched her hand towards the ruined figure with difficulty. "Pretty lady."

He turned away from the hideous thing. It reminded him too much of the real injuries he'd seen his comrades endure... or fail to endure.

The next shop was a small supermarket. He

pushed the broken door back on its hinges and went inside, thinking here might be something of use to add to their meagre rations.

But a quick glance revealed the shop had been almost entirely looted. There was nothing left of any use.

On one counter was a bottle trapped inside a cast of dust. He recognised the distinctive shape as a popular brand of gin. Yet it seemed unopened; a prisoner in the past. It seemed a shame to disturb it, so he let it stay in its dream of a world before the war. He wished dearly that he could join it.

Standing in the street, he took a moment to orientate himself. The map he held in his head was of limited use, but he had an idea of the direction they needed to head in.

The city's streets had always been pretty dirty and gritty, but now they had been oddly transformed. They'd become emaciated, it seemed to him. Preyed upon by unkempt vegetation for so long that they were merely hollowed-out shells.

The autumn winds made the dead leaves dance along the cracked pavements, as if leading them both on.

They came to a street that he was sure would bring them nearer to their goal. It looked relatively easy to navigate, which was a bonus.

Within a few minutes of setting off, he began to doubt that he'd made the right choice.

Almost as soon as they'd started walking, he'd noticed that every door and ground-floor window had been bricked up. He doubted the fleeing residents were responsible for that, so he assumed the local or military authorities had been responsible. Though he couldn't think why they would bother, or where they would find the time and resources to carry out the work.

The blindness of the houses hadn't been obvious in the gloom.

The street was quite narrow and the houses felt pinched together. Certainly there was no room for more than one car to pass another.

The end of the street was shrouded in light morning mist, but he could just make out that it curved slightly to the right.

When they eventually reached that point, he'd expected the street to open out onto other streets. Instead it curved back towards the left and then stretched straight ahead for several hundred yards before curving again.

Had he unwittingly blundered into a maze, he wondered, but reminded himself that it hadn't been obvious from the map he'd studied yesterday.

There were no streets leading off either right or left. They hadn't seen any since they'd begun walking.

She stirred on his back. "I don't like this place, daddy."

He produced a fake chuckle for her benefit. "But why not, sweetheart? It's just a street." The grey, blank faces of the houses stared at him with reproach.

"No, it's not. It's not nice," she said.

He noticed suddenly on his left that one of the bricked up doors had been broken open. He pointed it out to her. "Let's have a look, shall we?"

Approaching the house slowly, he became very aware of the sound his boots made, crunching on the road. When they were nearly at the open door he looked around carefully. He was hoping to find out if the door had been smashed in, or whether someone had broken out. But it wasn't obvious.

Now they were standing right in font of the opening. They could see that there was a space of about two or three feet before a near-vertical hillside of rubble blocked their way. He'd have struggled to climb it on his own, but it would be impossible while he was carrying her.

"We'd best carry on, eh?" was the best he could offer her. He knew that if they encountered anyone – or anything – here they'd be trapped.

The street curved and twisted around a central axis. He was sure that he'd tramped along it for over a mile by now.

The ground beneath his feet was turning from tarmac and paving to a dirty grey mud. His progress became harder and harder. He began to sweat again.

He was about to suggest that she get down off his back for a short while when he spotted a narrow alley leading off to the left. It was crammed in between two houses, and was hardly wide enough for two people walking side by side, but it gave him a sense of relief a mile wide.

He nodded his head in that direction. "Let's try down there, shall we?"

He struggled over to the gap and was about to walk down it when he saw a figure walking towards them. He watched carefully as it stumbled a step or two, then leant against the wall.

Unsure what to do, he stood and watched for a few moments longer. His sense of decency finally overwhelmed him. "Are you all right?" he asked. "Do you need some help?"

The figure started at the sound of his voice, almost losing balance. "Hello? Hello?"

"We're here," he said, stretching out to touch the man's arm. He saw that the man's eye was covered by a cataract. He probably couldn't see them at all.

Then the man turned his head and he saw that his other eye was missing. Even though he'd seen much worse during the war, it caused him to shrink back. The eye was grey and dead. It looked as if skin had grown over it. Then part of it moved.

"Have you seen my friends?" asked the man. "They said they'd be back a long time ago. Days ago..."

"No. No, I haven't, sorry." He peered at the man's eye and saw that part of it was made up of fleshy fronds, waving in the air slowly as if sensing something.

The man nodded in resignation. "Thank you." He limped away, one hand against the wall.

They continued walking for a few more seconds. The alley was claustrophobic but soon gave way to an open space.

They'd arrived at an enclosed square at the rear of several blank-faced buildings, with red brick and concrete jostling for position.

He assumed that the place had probably been used as a makeshift hospital during the war. The medical staff had clearly abandoned it along with the remaining patients.

To one side of the crowded square was a miniature forest of crutches, braces and other surgical aids. They leaned against the wall like some bizarre sculpture, waiting to be appreciated by an absent crowd of sophisticates.

They must belong to the people he saw before him, who filled up the square. They all appeared as if they had the same deformity as the man. It was as if they'd been cured of one affliction, only to be visited by one far worse.

Figures slumped everywhere, covering the ground. The place was a graveyard for the living. The stench was appalling.

He began to pick his way carefully, making for another alleyway on the far side of the square.

One or two people were on their feet, mainly near the walls. One girl stood near to them and seemed to sense their presence. Perhaps she can smell that we're different he thought. Though how she smelled anything other than the thick stench of the place puzzled him.

"Please... please... can you help me?" Her face was pointing slightly away from them.

He coughed, then asked "What is it you want?"

He was startled when the girl turned her face towards the sound.

What looked like dozens of tiny worms were crawling under her livid skin, burrowing deeply then re-appearing in an endless rhythm. Like the eyes of the man they'd spoken to a moment ago, hers too seemed changed in some way.

Her hand was suddenly on his arm. "Have you seen my father? I'm sure he came this way."

He was about to answer, and had begun to raise him arm to point towards the alleyway, but then halted. Could she see in some way despite her malformed eyes? Maybe she could see different things...

"J-just keep going the way you're headed. We just passed him."

She nodded and looked up at him. "Thank you."

He wondered what she was seeing. Her fingers stayed where they were for several seconds too long, he felt. Then she let go of his arm and walked away, slowly and carefully.

Hearing the exchange, the others in the square were now struggling to their feet. Whereas before they had ignored him and Mari, now they all turned to face them. He estimated there must have been over a hundred people crammed into the small, dark square. No-one said anything, but the crowd began to move in their direction.

With their odd eye deformities, he wasn't sure if the people could see them – maybe they sensed the two of them some other way. Either way, he didn't feel comfortable with the situation. Unlike the two people they'd met already, everyone here was silent.

Suddenly they were too close. An arm grabbed his sleeve and tugged. Then another followed it. Soon there was a wall of hands reaching for them. Mari began to make whimpering noises, clearly afraid.

Some hands grabbed and others clawed, while some merely waved in the air aimlessly, complementing and contradicting each other in an endless, meaningless rhythm. He put his head down and pushed through them, not daring to stop for fear of becoming one of them, or of abandoning his daughter to them.

Not one of them made any sound beyond the slightest of sighs. Somehow that made it all worse.

He winced as Mari screamed in his ear. "Daddy! Daddeee! What do they want!?"

"I don't know. Just hang on tight to me, OK?" He scanned the building nearest to them. There was a drainpipe and a deep window ledge that might provide some respite. But first they had to get there.

He began bringing his large fists down on the heads and faces of the people in his way. It was cruel, he knew, but he couldn't think of any other way to save Mari. Once or twice he was sure he heard bones cracking.

Panting hard, they finally reached the wall. He grabbed the sturdy metal drainpipe and tested it. It would take their weight, thankfully.

Soon they were several feet off the ground.

Mari sobbed into his ear as he swung over to the left and planted his boot firmly on the wide ledge. It was wide enough to stand on with room to spare, but it would take a feat of balance not to topple back into the clawing crowd below.

"Here we go, sweetheart. Grip tight now!" He swung himself round, releasing his grip on the drainpipe and rotating them swiftly onto the ledge. He watched as their supply pack slipped off his arm and knocked two people below off their feet.

"Damn!" he cursed to himself. Now they had no food or water. But at least they were safe from the crowd below.

Standing sideways, he looked longingly at the alleyway they needed to reach. He cursed himself for backing them into this corner. Escape might as well be a hundred miles away.

"Are you OK, Mari?" he whispered.

"Yes, Daddy." He felt the fingers of her one hand digging into his back in fright.

He undid the two wide straps on her harness. "It's OK. You can let go now. We're safe here for a while." He hoped his words were true. The crowd below were still clawing the air in their direction. None of them had tried to scale the drainpipe yet, but he couldn't help wondering if it was just a matter of time.

He set Mari down at his side. There was enough room for her to sit sideways, with just one foot hanging over the edge of the windowsill.

"Comfy?" he asked, with a smile. She nodded.

He squatted on the ledge. His thoughts turned to a means of escaping from their predicament.

Perhaps they could break the window and escape inside the building, he thought. But what waited for them inside might be even worse.

He peered in through the grime covering the window. There was some sort of mesh on the inside of the glass that made seeing inside even more difficult. Gradually his eyes became used to the gloom, and he realised he was looking at a room that had probably once been an office.

Now it appeared to be a temporary ward of some sort. There were two beds in the room and he could see part of the way down a corridor that had several gurneys lined up on one side.

Then he realised suddenly that the beds were occupied. He rubbed at the dirt covering the window to gain a better view. A foot was handcuffed to the bed frame nearest to him. The body in the other bed, which was similarly chained, was missing several parts. The cut marks on the flesh and bone looked rough and hasty; far less than surgical. There were numerous dark patches on the floor, which he guessed must be blood.

He caught his breath as he realised with a shock that what he was looking at wasn't a medical ward but a larder. His neck muscles tightened at the thought that the people filling the square had resorted to cannibalism to survive. Now he knew exactly what they wanted from him and Mari.

He ruled out breaking the window. The mesh inside was probably too strong to break anyway.

When he returned his attention to the crowd below, he noticed that many of them had lost interest in him and Mari. Many had turned their backs on them and some had even returned to their slumped positions on the ground.

His wife's voice was in his head again, remonstrating with him for getting himself and their daughter into such a mess. He nodded, as if listening carefully.

As the afternoon wore on, dusk seemed to fall

on the narrow square ahead of everywhere else. Through the alleyway that he longed to walk down, he could see it was still relatively bright daylight.

He had no idea how well the people below him could see, or even if they could see at all, but he knew that bad light was an ally he could rely on.

He leaned over to his daughter, who was slumped dozing, and whispered "Time we were on our way." She looked up at him with bleary, frightened eyes and he nodded in reassurance.

Strapping the harness back in place and making sure Mari was comfortable, he stood with his face to the window and took a deep breath. Going down on one knee, he swung his other leg out over the ledge, gripping the sill's edge at the same time. With one swift move, he let himself down so that he was hanging from the ledge by his hands.

Mari sucked in her breath as he began to move from side to side like a pendulum. The ground was about seven feet below them now. He had to time this right.

Suddenly, as they swung in the direction of the alley, he let himself drop. Their fall was broken by a couple of patients dozing against the wall. They wailed in distress, alerting the others. But by then he was on his feet and running for the narrow slit of the alleyway.

Hands reached out for them ineffectually. Two figures moved between him and his goal, but he simply shrugged them out of the way. By now a dozen of them were on their feet and heading to intercept him and his daughter.

But the gap between the buildings opened up to welcome them, and the sound of his running feet hammered back at them from two brick walls. Within a minute they were through to the other side and into a street filled with rubble. He kept up the momentum as best he could without taking a tumble over bits of wrecked houses.

He slowed enough to risk a glance backwards. The patients had reached as far as the end of the alley but seemed unwilling to follow him. Did they know something he didn't? He had no idea if they had some disease, or whether they were victims of a horrific experiment, but he was glad to be away from them.

Bending forward with his hands on his knees, he panted heavily. He wasn't as fit as when he'd been a soldier, that was for sure.

"Are you OK, sweetheart?" he asked, between huge breaths. He felt Mari's small hand tug at one of his ears gently. "Yes, thank you, Daddy. This is good. I'm glad we got away from there. Those people scared me."

He nodded in agreement. "We're safe now, sweetheart. We'll be OK."

~

The afternoon was drawing on as they skirted the centre of the city. The fighting had been fierce here. He remembered being pinned down near the railway station for over a day by enemy fire.

He tried to push his memories to the back of his head as they passed the ruins of the grand 19th-century station and headed in the direction of one of the more prosperous suburbs.

A number of hotels were clustered near the station. Most had disappeared into the rubble, but one or two had been lucky enough to survive more or less intact.

Standing at the top of the steps to a Brutalist-style hotel was a man dressed in a blue suit and a dark coat. He had a long face topped with greasy-looking, untidy hair.

He stopped and looked up at the strange man, who seemed completely out of place in this ruin of luxury. Just in case the man was an illusion, he closed his eyes for a second. The man insisted on being there when he opened them again.

"Good afternoon!" said the stranger. "It's been a nice day, hasn't it?"

It hadn't been anything resembling a nice day but, unaccustomed to such civility in this decidedly barbarous place, he was caught off guard. "Yes," he replied, without conviction.

"Who is he, Daddy?" whispered his daughter. He just shook his head. It was the only honest thing he could do. When he ran out of bright ideas, he was surprised to find himself falling back on honesty – at least it was a lot less work that way.

"Will you join me for coffee?" asked the man. "It's freshly made."

Coffee? For the past three months they'd been making do with water, and something that said 'Tea' on the packet, but which tasted like disappointing dust once brewed.

He could do with some decent caffeine right now. He nodded his head eagerly and then, remembering his manners, tacked a grateful "Yes, please" on the end of it.

He walked up to where the man stood smiling at them. "It's unusual to have company nowadays," the stranger said, softly.

The coffee might be poisoned, of course, or this might be a trap of some sort. Or the sky might fall on him. Or a million other things. "Thank you," he said and wearily followed the man through the large revolving door. This had been one of the more expensive hotels in the city. He'd never been in here before.

"The lift no longer works but it's only one flight up," said the man, heading for the wide staircase at the rear of the lobby. "My name is Theo Harbilt, by the way."

"Do you live here, Mr Harbilt?"

"Just Theo will do. I dislike honorifics like Mr... or Doctor... or Professor..."

There was no way of knowing whether Harbilt could claim either of the last two titles but he just nodded. He also noticed that Harbilt had avoided answering the question. The thought occurred to him that maybe the man had been a politician before the war. And that maybe he still was.

He led them along a gloomy corridor until they came to impressive-looking double doors at the end. They were unlocked and Harbilt swung them open with a flourish, revealing a large living space.

The room was decorated in a style that used lots of chrome. There was a large animal skin in the middle of the floor. He couldn't identify the beast that had 'donated' it, but he felt sure he'd never seen a live example.

Instead of art or photographs hanging on the walls, Harbilt had several strange illustrations and technical diagrams instead. He looked at one or two for a while but they were indecipherable to him.

He undid the straps, and Mari sat down on one of the big modern armchairs arranged around a glass coffee table.

Harbilt had disappeared, so they sat enjoying the comfort of the chairs. Shortly, their host appeared carrying a tray filled with coffee, fruit juices and cakes.

Mari stared hungrily at the cakes. As soon as Harbilt placed the plate on the arm of her chair, she grabbed the delicacy and crammed it into her mouth. Crumbs rained down all around her.

"Mari. Remember your manners," said her father, mildly.

Harbilt smiled. "It really doesn't matter. As long as you're enjoying it, Mari."

The girl nodded and tried to say 'thank you' through a cake-filled mouth. Her father sighed meaningfully.

He warily accepted a cup of coffee but declined a cake. It was only when he saw Harbilt drink from the same pot of coffee that he thought it safe to drink some himself.

"It's good coffee. Thank you. I haven't tasted any in a while."

Harbilt merely smiled back.

"So do you live here? In this hotel?" he asked. It was odd to see such luxury among the devastation.

"For the time being, yes. I'm an engineer by profession but you could say I'm temporarily acting as a government observer."

A frown crawled across his brow. "Really – which government?"

"Well, the *real* government, of course. The one you fought for!"

He snorted at the reply. He had only fought for them because of an accident of geography –

he had no idea how 'real' they were. "I see. And what are you observing for them?"

Harbilt shook his head. "I can't tell you that, I'm afraid. I really can't." He rattled his cup down on the coffee table as if to underline his seriousness.

Silence reigned for a few minutes before Harbilt seemed as though he could no longer stand it.

"Forgive me... uh..." Harbilt paused as if eliciting information.

"Lieutenant." He thought it best to continue the fiction. Their host seemed like someone to whom status was important. It was also a good way to avoid giving away any other information.

"Lieutenant, yes. Forgive me, but why are you in the city? No doubt you are currently on some sort of mission yourself..." He followed his insult with a short chuckle that nodded in the direction of malevolence.

He glanced at his daughter before answering. "We're going to visit my wife's grave. But we've been delayed a few times. We've seen some very odd things."

Harbilt moved to the edge of his chair. "Odd in what way?"

He swallowed another mouthful of coffee. It seemed to have sharpened his wits and driven away the tiredness. "We saw some huge machines. They were like enormous crabs that were searching for something in the rubble. That is, I *think* they were machines... "

"Ah, I see. I think you mean the collectors. They've been operating in the city again for the last few days," said Harbilt.

"You seem to know a lot about them."

The man smiled with pleasure. "You could say they were my idea," he said.

"What do you mean? What are they exactly?"

Harbilt beamed at the show of curiosity. "They're a kind of armoured vehicle, designed to go where normal tracked or wheeled vehicles can't go. I got the idea while watching a film of mountain goats clambering up and down impossibly steep slopes. And they refuel as they go along, by gathering anything of use to 'burn' in on-board fuel cells.

"They're controlled by the mind – or the soul, if you prefer to think of it that way – of a deceased soldier. I'm no biologist, though. The complicated bits were done by the Ministry scientists. I was just a... consultant, you could say."

The thought sent a shiver through the 'Lieutenant'. In his disgust and horror, he thought of the knife tucked into his boot. "You mean there's a corpse inside each of those *things?*"

"Oh no. No, not at all. They're controlled remotely. I believe the bodies are stored cryogenically while the brains are... um, accessed."

Fighting back the urge to retch, he stood up and walked to the window. A darkness gripped him, and he struggled to fight it. Knowing that he was in the presence of the man who dreamt up those terrifying things made him feel contaminated.

Sensing that he'd made his guest uncomfortable, Harbilt attempted some mild flattery. "I'm sure you'll agree, Lieutenant, that soldiers' minds are well-disciplined and obedient."

His thoughts returned to the knife. "And who are they obedient to?"

Harbilt seemed lost for a moment. "Well, ultimately... someone in the higher echelons of the government, I'd imagine."

It was obvious that the man didn't care who

or what was controlling those things. They'd bought him a privileged life and that was all he cared about.

"They killed a young boy earlier today!" He spat the words at the complacent fool.

Harbilt's face dropped. He shook his head. "No. No, that can't be right. You must be mistaken. They're not allowed to do that, I'm sure. You must be mistaken. They're designed for reconnaissance and rescue."

He wasn't used to doubt but it crept into his thoughts now. All he'd seen for certain was the collectors pursuing the boy. He'd only heard what he thought was the boy's death at their... 'hands'. It wasn't enough to press things any further.

"Hmmmm. Well..." was his feeble reply.

If, as he claimed, Harbilt was working in some way for the government that he and his comrades had fought to save, then they were very wrong. He felt guilty by association. Maybe he'd been fighting on the wrong side, after all.

He wanted to slap the man's stupid face, but he was afraid he'd never be able to wash the filth away if he touched him. Inside, Harbilt was a moral cripple.

He stared out into the darkness beyond the glass. It had become dark too quickly and he wished he'd never set foot in this damned hotel.

His host noticed that night had fallen. "You can't leave now. You must stay the night. I have several spare rooms."

He would feel dirty if he accepted Harbilt's offer, but Mari couldn't sleep in the open. The journey had taken much longer than he'd thought it would. He'd imagined they could reach their destination and return within a day. Reluctantly, he accepted the offer for his daughter's sake.

Harbilt showed them into a large room with a double bed. "Will this do? Or would Mari prefer a separate room?"

"This is fine, thank you." He wanted to be able to keep an eye on his daughter. He didn't want them divided and conquered.

"Please feel free to take a bath if you want to," Harbilt offered.

"You have running water?" he said in surprise.

Harbilt nodded. "Yes, the army looks after me quite well. As far as they're concerned, I have my uses, so I'm worth looking after."

"Hmmmm," he grunted.

After helping Mari to bathe and putting her to bed, he stepped out onto the small balcony. Darkness had fallen over the ruined suburbs. A dog barked somewhere. Tomorrow would have to do to continue on their way.

A shower was appealing, but he didn't like being vulnerable in a strange place, so he simply stripped to his shorts and t-shirt and climbed into bed.

He found no rest in his fitful dream-punctured sleep. In his dream, great thick-legged things marched across the city. They had the eyes of children, blackened hearts and no soul. And they were all coming to claim him and drag him off to their frost-covered hell.

He lay in the greyish gloom, panting and staring at the shapes he thought he saw moving across the ceiling.

Just after dawn, he left Harbilt's suite and climbed the remaining stairs as far as he could, his binoculars slung around his neck.

From a largely intact room on the ninth floor he could see out towards the cemetery. The road looked fairly clear. Closer to the hotel, he spotted several cars that they might be able to use to travel the remaining few miles.

Back in the suite, he satisfied himself that his daughter was still asleep before slipping out to recce for a still serviceable vehicle.

Out on the street, a thin cold mist hung sluggishly around his boots. His breath made clouds for him to walk through.

He'd only walked around the block from the hotel when he came across an old machine gun post nestled on a street corner. The wall behind it was decorated with bullet holes and there were scorch marks on the ground in front.

Out of idle curiosity, he clambered over the burst sandbags to peer inside. The rusting barrel of a heavy machine gun pointed at him accusingly. If anyone had died in here, their comrades had dragged the bodies away.

He was about to continue his journey when a bullet sang past his head and thumped into the wall behind him.

Instinctively, he leapt behind the old sandbags and covered his head. He didn't think a sniper would waste his time or ammunition in a de-populated city, so he thought the shooter would be relatively easy to spot.

Cautiously, he peered through the narrow gap between the wall and a sandbag. There was a figure standing in full view, walking forward stiffly, rifle raised ready to fire.

He glanced around on the floor, quickly. Just behind his left foot was an assault rifle.

A bullet tore into the wall a foot from his head, dislodging small chunks of masonry. He'd sworn at the end of the war that he'd never pick up a gun again, but now he had no choice.

He picked up the assault rifle and pulled the magazine from its slot. Assuring himself that it was almost full, he pushed it back into place. Almost immediately, all the metal parts of the gun began to come apart. Several screws fell to the floor, clearly heavily rusted. The barrel followed them, along with other vital parts of the weapon.

It was as if the gun had suddenly decayed rapidly in his hands. Maybe it was making up for lost time since the end of the war. Maybe it was missing the soft caress of a soldier's hands. Or perhaps it just sensed his current distaste for firearms and felt insulted. He almost chuckled at the absurdity of it.

"Why the hell can't that happen to *his* gun?" he growled to himself.

Eventually he was left holding just the wooden stock. He gripped it tightly, desperately.

It was now his only means of defence. Even without the weight of a gun behind it, a wooden stock could still stop a man in his tracks. All he had to do now was live long enough to use it.

The scarecrow of a soldier was still advancing on him, with his gun raised in menace. He didn't understand why the man hadn't already felled him with a bullet. Perhaps he had no ammunition left.

Almost at once, four loud reports put paid to that forlorn hope. He ducked down behind the sandbags as a loud rumble filled the air, growing in intensity as a cloud of dust rolled quickly into the remains of the machine gun nest. Burying his face in his arms, he sat and waited for the dust to settle as the echoes faded away.

After a minute or two, he scrambled to his feet and peered out at the street. There was no sign of the soldier. He presumed the deranged combatant now lay under the impressive pile of masonry that filled the place where he had last stood. The vibration of gunfire so close was too much for the fragile walls, which had tumbled onto him, like a mini Jericho.

Sympathy was the last thing on his mind, but he began to clamber carefully over the tumbled wreckage. Spotting the edge of a sleeve, he cleared away the stones one by one until he reached the man's head. Beneath the dust-caked hair lay a large hole in the man's right temple. The darkness visible within seemed to go on forever. Despite the huge load that had just crushed him, there was not a single drop of blood anywhere. A greenish-black liquid began to leak from the man's dead eyes.

The desiccated skin appalled him. It looked as if it hadn't been alive for quite some time. Could this soldier be another of Harbilt's disgusting experiments?

He pulled both his hands away quickly and stood up. Suddenly he became afraid that the darkness leaking from the husk of humanity before him might infect him, claim him somehow.

Placing his boots carefully, he clambered down to flatter ground and dusted himself off. The thing was better off buried. It looked like it should have been buried a long time ago.

~

The car was comfortable inside. It had clearly been an expensive toy, but it might as well be an old wooden cart as far as he was concerned. As long as it got them where they were going.

The permit on the glass showed it had once been a government car. He didn't know why it had been abandoned and didn't care. Given his recent history with borrowed vehicles, he hoped it worked.

Seated behind the wheel, he searched for the keys. They weren't in the ignition but a quick search uncovered a spare set hidden in the passenger side sun visor. Very sloppy, he thought.

The mirror on the visor reflected a grey canvas bag on the back seat. He reached back to lift it up but stopped a few inches short. The bag was deformed in a way that suggested it held a human head.

He got out and opened the back door. The bag had a large blood stain on the side and some had leaked onto the seat. He carefully picked it up and left it at the side of the road. "Sorry there's no time for a funeral," he muttered.

Back behind the wheel, he found that the big car started first time and its engine sounded well-tuned and happy. He was glad to see there was plenty of fuel in it, too.

He carefully negotiated the debris-strewn streets back to the hotel, making sure to park the car where it wouldn't be seen from the windows of Harbilt's suite.

Creeping softly to where Mari was sleeping, he woke her gently. She looked at him in confusion.

"We're leaving now, sweetheart. I've found us a car. C'mon, time to saddle up!" His voice was little more than a murmur. He didn't want to wake their host.

Downstairs, he carefully strapped Mari into her seat. She smiled and ran her hand over the soft leather. "It's nice."

He climbed into the driver's seat and pointed the car in the direction of the cemetery.

The road was relatively uncluttered by debris. Despite the attempts of the plant life to break up the tarmac, he found it a relatively smooth drive. To one side, a row of trees still stood, overshadowing the road. If he squinted, he could almost see it as it had been before the fighting started.

A drift of browned leaves took off in the car's slipstream, performing a complex shimmy in honour of its passage.

He tried to remember the route to the cemetery. Most of it was clear in his mind, but there was the odd small gap. He kept his eyes open for the right turning.

The irony of seeking a graveyard in a city that had itself become a necropolis wasn't lost on him, as he caught sight of a bent road sign pointing the way.

Within a few minutes, the sight of graves covering a small hill appeared on the left hand side. He slowed the car, peering cautiously as they pulled up outside the main entrance. The skin at the back of his neck crawled. The dead were no threat, he told himself. It was the living who had always caused him problems.

The gates had been displaced and deformed by a large explosion. Much of the charred paint had since flaked off in the rain. Now they simply looked like bizarre sculptures, abandoned inconveniently between two gateposts.

He got Mari ready. They made their way cautiously between the large metal obstacles.

Inside, the cemetery was pock-marked with shell holes. Pieces of shattered headstone lay here and there, with fragments of bone and body in between them.

He surveyed the scene with horror. "They died a second death," he muttered to himself.

"What, Daddy? What did you say?"

He shook his head. He seemed to be doing a lot of that these days. "Nothing, sweetie. Don't worry," he lied. He did a lot of that, too.

Something in the corner of his eyes made him turn quickly. A dark figure, wrapped in rags, sat with its back against a broken gravestone, unmoving.

"Hey, hello," he called. Still the figure remained motionless. Maybe it hadn't heard or was in too deep a slumber to respond.

Cautiously he walked over to the figure and touched its shoulder, ready to retreat quickly. Again there was no response, so he reached forward to pull back the ragged hood that hid the figure's face.

Beneath the hood, a toothsome rictus of death smiled back at him. The flesh on the face had either withered or been eaten away.

Mari made a disgusted noise, so he quickly flicked the hood back into place. Leaving the corpse to guard the dead, they began to climb the path leading to the top of the cemetery.

Past the churned-up ground at the bottom of

the hill, the cemetery was much more intact. Up here there was only the odd smashed monument or a gravestone grazed by a stray bullet.

His memory led him to the far corner of the burial ground, where the graves were sheltered by the shade of several old, black trees. Their branches spread like a canopy over the dozen or so burial plots tucked away near the crumbling wall.

"Here it is," he said, unbuckling the harness and letting his daughter down.

The plain grey headstone bore the name Arina Hearn and her dates. A fancy inscription had seemed so inappropriate at the time. What he wanted to say now would never fit in a space so small.

Mari dragged herself to the stone and began to run her fingers over the letters of her mother's name. "Will we dig her up, Daddy?" she asked.

"What?! No! No!" He didn't want his daughter to see the changes that seven years in the grave had wrought on his wife. He didn't want to see it himself. He couldn't stand that. "That would be wrong."

Mari's large eyes gazed up at him. Tears shone on her cheeks. "But she said she was going to help me," she said, plaintively.

He bent and put his hand on her shoulder. "She's been gone a long time, Mari. I don't think she can help anyone now."

As he stepped forward to brush some crisped leaves from the top of the gravestone, his foot hit something. It had been hidden at first by a drift of fallen leaves, but he kicked them away with his boot.

What looked like a thin, gnarled root extended from the ground near the gravestone. It ended in a large white object nestling among the roots of a tree a few yards away. The rounded object looked like a huge fungus, feeding from the tree to which it clung. But he knew that wasn't the truth.

Kneeling next to it, he tugged gently at the wet, papery surface. It peeled away without much effort, revealing the almost transparent sac inside.

His daughter had crawled laboriously over to him and was now almost at his side. Despite the huge size of the creature inside, its features told her what she needed to know. "It's me, isn't it?"

He nodded. It was his daughter, yes. But it was a version without the wounds inflicted on her in the womb. "Your mother still dreams you in her death."

Or you as you would have been he thought. He looked down at his daughter with her withered legs and distorted face, scarred and partly frozen by shrapnel. Hair covered only half of her scalp and she was too small for a girl of her age.

The child is still alive. But there is so little of her.

He saw the scars of her own battles since birth, some hidden beneath her clothes but others visible on her neck and arms. Her several suicide attempts had left him shaken, unsure of how to treat her. He'd had no idea children as young as her even thought about suicide. There were many times he'd been scared to leave her on her own, but the necessity of finding food or other supplies had forced him to trust her.

Binding her wounds after one attempt, he'd vowed that he'd do everything he could to make things right for her. His failure stared him in the face every time he caught sight of her scarred skin.

He'd seen too many people die when they desperately wanted to live. He didn't know how to talk to someone who sought death out.

His time in the army had taught him plenty of ways to kill someone but he didn't know how to make them want to live.

Once, in a fit of anger, his wife had called him a 'stupid soldier'. At the time, he'd bridled at the description, but as time passed, he agreed with her comment more and more.

The worst thing was that he could do nothing to help his daughter. He felt like a fraud, an empty thing, his soul worn threadbare by years of sorrow and worry.

He looked at his daughter, wanting to lift her up and change her life for the better in some miraculous act. Only his duty to her had kept him alive since his wife's death. Now that seemed like it wasn't nearly enough for either of them.

Mari grasped the root then looked at the bizarre facsimile of herself. She peered at it for a short while then up at her father. "Cut it, Daddy. Please cut it."

He looked down at her, not knowing if she understood what she was asking for. Her steady, determined gaze told him that she did. She clearly thought that she'd found a way for her mother to help her after all.

Somehow they both knew this was an act of finality. There were no signs, no warnings, but it was still very clear to them.

"Are you sure, sweetheart? Really sure..." He choked on his words.

The girl simply nodded. "I'm too broken, Daddy."

Now it seemed that, at last, he saw her for what she was; a flower that had been plucked and placed in a vase. Its bright face appeared to be alive but, in truth, it was already dead.

For a moment he hesitated, then, reaching down, he pulled the small knife from the scabbard tucked in his sock. Then he leant forward and began to saw at the fibrous root. It began to leak a clear liquid as the creature inside the rough sphere began to move. A high pitched moan filled the air as the root was finally severed with a gush of liquid.

"Thank you, Daddy," said Mari, then clutched at her stomach. She fluttered for a moment in his vision, like a moth, then was gone.

Everything wavered as the ground lurched downwards beneath his feet. He felt that the substance of his world had been suddenly thinned out, leaking away into nowhere.

Black scratching branches clawed the sky, trying desperately to hold on to something.

Everything around him began to collapse. The world was like a balloon being suddenly and catastrophically deflated.

Further down the slope of the burial ground, corpses were resurrected from their graves as the ground heaved beneath them, disgorging them to face a premature judgement day.

His feet went from under him as another tremor shook him loose. It looked to him like the cemetery was turning up on end.

He dug his fingers into the soil, but it had no substance, as if he was grasping at air. He started to slide backwards. The world began to close in on him, tumbling down upon him.

As her gravestone crumbled before his eyes, sections of it hurtling down past his head, he realised that his wife had been right all those years ago – he was just a stupid soldier. Otherwise he'd have gathered his daughter in his arms and fled this city long ago.

A stupid soldier. Who else would stay in a place hollowed out by war and kept alive only by a dead woman's dream?

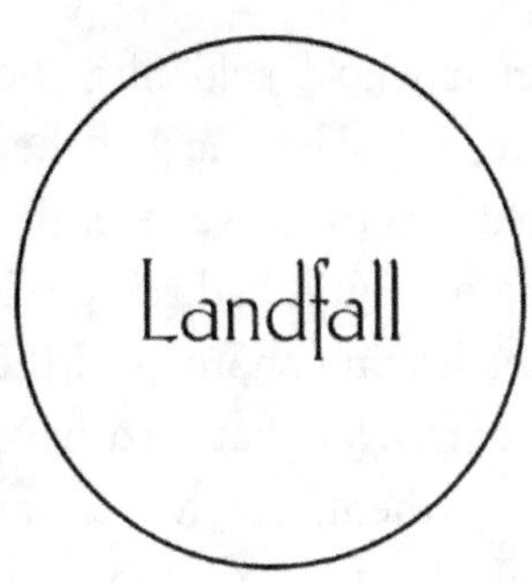

The tiny grey boat was a dot on a much larger canvas of darker grey. The darker colour stretched from shore to shore. But no shore was in sight any longer.

The channel was narrow. It should have been easy to cross it in little more than an hour. But they had been swept away from the land and now they were adrift, without any way back. They'd packed what food they could. That was nearly two days ago. It was barely enough for the journey, and not nearly enough for two days. The little that was left was now saturated with brine.

A night crossing was safer, everyone had said. He'd realised how empty those words were as he saw the few lights on the far shore drift off to the side, like departing ships on an uncertain, alien sea.

The woman who'd sold him the boat had seemed honest. Maybe she'd made a mistake when she told him there was plenty of petrol in the small engine. But it had run dry less than 15 minutes after leaving shore. And there was no sail and no oars. Not that he'd have been any good at using them. He was a farmer – he understood the land, not the sea.

They had run from the men with the guns. They lived on the plain overlooking the sea, so their eyes turned there when they sought escape. A boat could easily cross the channel – it looked only very narrow from where they stood. Safety lay on the other side. Safety... and his brother's family would take them in. But now it seemed death would be their only saviour.

For three years the men with guns had roamed unchecked across their land. For the previous two years the harvest had been poor. What little there was had been looted or burned by the fighters. This year there had been no harvest.

His neighbours had all faced hardship, too. Those that hadn't been killed had left the land, abandoning their farms and the years of hard work it had taken to build them. Some had joined the militias, he'd heard. He could never do that. Killing an animal was hard enough – to kill another man would have been impossible. It was obvious that few of his countrymen felt the same way.

When the militia had turned up at their farmhouse one day, the officer had dragged him round to the back of the house. He remembered the cold grey eyes of the young lieutenant as he had stuck a gun in his stomach and demanded his co-operation. His hard eyes were matched by his hard words, threats that struck to the core of his life. "We need soldiers. You will join our cause. You will fight and maybe die for us" the man in the grubby uniform had ordered. The officer's eyes had strayed to the rear window of the house. "Otherwise..."

Only when he had pleaded for the lives of his wife and child, tears streaming down his face, did the man stop poking him with the barrel of his gun and stalk away in disgust.

They had scraped together what money they could and tried to pay their way to safety. Their choice had been made after much agonising and now it seemed like a terrible thing that they had done.

His wife huddled in the prow of the tiny boat, trying in vain to shelter herself and their child from the wind and water. It was a hopeless task.

The boat rose and rocked as another big wave bucked under them. She moaned and clung tightly to the bundle in her arms.

He gazed out across the water as he gripped the side of the boat tightly. The sea looked like an endless series of unforgiving steel plates, melting and re-forming from second to second as they slid over and under one another in an endless, bleak ballet. There seemed no end to it, stretching away unbroken in whichever direction he looked. Despite the presence of his wife and son, he felt lonely and desolate.

Overhead the sky was a blanket of grey, growing darker as they watched. A storm was being prepared, they feared. When it arrived, their boat would be swamped. They would surely lose their lives.

They both watched the sky nervously for the next hour, but the grey mass of dark clouds stayed on the horizon, never creeping closer. As time passed, the clouds disappeared behind them and they gave praise for their rare good luck. The weather was on their side, for now.

He looked in pity on his wife and their infant son. He'd wanted to bring them to safety but instead he'd only led them to this lingering death. He had failed as both a husband and a father. He'd masqueraded as both but was successful only as an executioner. The unwelcome thought that perhaps it would have been better merely to surrender to the soldiers rose to the surface of his mind.

He'd thought the child would bring them joy among their despair. Instead his wife's troubled pregnancy, the lack of medicines and the boy's sickly appearance had been an unending source of worry. Even if there had been enough to eat, he was sure he'd have lost weight during those fretful days, his mind weighed down and wearied by desperation.

The wind had picked up now. Despite choosing the summer for their crossing, the wind and water were wilder than he'd expected. He'd often gazed out over the summer sea from his vantage point over the water and thought how calm and blue it looked. He could only think that they'd left it too late in the season to make their escape.

His wife was doing her best to protect their

child but sometimes it seemed hopeless. Despite her efforts to protect her son, he was feeding on as much salty spray as milk. She feared he might grow to be partly sea creature, cursed to dwell close to the shore forever.

Weariness now gnawed them to the bone. They'd struggled to stay awake in case some form of salvation came and went, completely unknown to them, while they slept. The hours rolled by monotonously until, despite their efforts, neither of them could stay awake any longer.

They slept fitfully, lulled partly by the slap and slop of the calmer waters against the boat's side. The baby cried out little during the course of the night and its mother feared it was growing weak.

The dawn revealed no respite from the unending grey leviathan on whose back they rode. Only the endless bowl of sky and the rising and falling ribbon of sea met their gaze. Even the rising sun seemed leached of any colour.

They had not eaten for so long. His wife was beginning to look ill. She was dry. "I have none for you," she whispered to the top of the crying baby's head.

For a moment she thought of drowning him... now, quickly. She could not bear to see him starve slowly. A quick sacrifice – a desperate, defiant gesture – would surely be better than waiting for the boy to be snatched away later by the beast that had them in its cruel grasp.

The sea was calmer now, though still more turbulent than he'd have liked. He squinted, struggling to see something that stood out from the blue and grey all around it. Patches of white bobbed into view every second or so. Whatever it was, it might offer some small salvation.

"Maybe there is food there," he murmured to himself. Plunging his arms into the sea, he pulled against the weight of the water. Slowly the boat began to move in the direction of the mass.

As the grey-green waters hid and then revealed their rotting treasure in turn, the carcass appeared to change shape, chunks of moribund flesh rising and falling on the surface. Now he could see it had been largely devoured, torn to pieces by dozens of ravenous mouths. It was writhing with eel-like fish.

As they came closer, the wind changed

direction, bringing with it the stink of piscine rot. Although his stomach was empty, he couldn't stop himself from retching at the stench.

There was nothing here for them, he realised. Whatever it had been in life, it had been too long dead. His wife groaned and leaned her head over the side.

He struggled to paddle the boat away from the rotten thing. His arms ached, feeling like they were being pulled out at the shoulders. Eventually the tide took hold of them and moved them away from the decaying mass.

He dozed, fatigue and despair getting the better of him. He woke only when his hand dropped over the side of the boat and trailed in the sea. He straightened, suddenly aware, and looked about him. Nothing had changed. His wife dozed with the child in her arms. At least when they slept they could escape their hunger for a while.

Slipping once more into uneasy sleep, he saw his father sitting in the boat with him. His face was angry, and he cursed his son for leaving the land. His father told him of how he and his own father had struggled to build it up, to make it fertile. It was a story he'd told his son a thousand times but, as he did so, he reached down into the boat and picked up two fistfuls of loamy soil and thrust them forward. "How could you leave this behind for a salty death?" he asked, before stretching his hands over the side of the boat and letting the earth fall between his fingers. It gathered on the surface in small islands for a moment before becoming waterlogged and sinking.

Jerking awake, he turned to reach out to the last few small clods of earth to rescue them from the water. But they had already melted away into dream.

Overwhelming despair descended on him. He had not only betrayed his wife and son but those who had come before him, too. He had paid them no thought and shown them nothing but disdain and dishonour.

Raising his head for a moment, he saw a dark shape against the brightening greyness of the sky. At first he imagined it must be a huge fish of some sort, and panic gripped him as he thought the creature saw them as food.

But then his mind cleared, and he realised it was a ship, much bigger and safer than their tiny boat.

Carefully he stood up in the boat, steadying himself as best he could so as not to tip it over, crying out to his wife to look. The smoke rising from the ship's funnel grew darker as it drew nearer, and he was sure the crew must have seen him.

The bulk of the ship seemed to dwarf them when it was still some distance away. He feared that the huge mass of the ship might crush their fragile boat like a whale unaware of the smaller fish that swam around it. But what other choice did they have than to seek help from this huge metal creature?

The vessel seemed to slow as it drew nearer and nearer. At last it pulled alongside them, but the sea refused to help, tossing and heaving the boat, threatening to smash it against the steel hull.

The wash from the larger vessel grew less with each second and he saw men busying themselves on the deck that towered over his head.

He stood and waved as rope nets were lowered over the side of the ship. A man on the deck was yelling instructions, either to him or the sailors on the scramble nets. He understood the language but the words were torn away by the wind.

The sea rolled under them, dashing their fragile boat against the ship's side. He feared that the boat would splinter, snatching safety from them when it was so close. Thinking only of his wife and son, he knelt and grabbed them, thrusting them into the grasp of the sailors reaching down to help them. Strong arms enfolded them, heaving them up to safety.

Another man was gesturing to him. He began to clamber unsteadily to his feet but the sea rocked the fragile boat again and he lurched forward. The huge bulk of the ship came to meet him and he plunged into a wave of darkness.

~

"Where am I?" His voice sounded hoarse and thin.

A face swung into view. it was moustachioed and self-assured. "Now, where do you want to be?" it asked.

He raised his head slightly and scanned his disorderly surroundings. "...not here," he croaked. It was the first thing that came to mind.

"Ah, that's a shame, because that's precisely where you are, you see. And damned ungrateful, it seems. Perhaps we should throw you back, eh?"

Another voice cut in, silencing the first man. "He's concussed – doesn't know what he's saying. Out of the way please, Mister Mate, and let me see to him."

The man leaned closer, dipping into a black leather bag. Pulling out various silver devices in turn the man pointed them at him before seeming satisfied. "You'll be fine. Just rest as much as you can. It'll hurt for a while but the skin isn't broken," he pronounced before disappearing.

Now he had time to look around, he searched quickly for his wife and son. Through an open hatchway he saw them seated at a table; she was feeding the boy some milk.

Ignoring the doctor's advice, he forced himself to his feet and made his way through the door. He sat opposite and reached out to stroke her hand. His wife gave him a weary smile before turning her attention back to the baby.

She used a small spoon to dribble the warm milk down her breast and into the baby's mouth.

It sucked hungrily at the food. When he'd had enough he gurgled, belched and smiled.

She had just laid the baby down on a makeshift cot that the cook had made for the child when the uniformed man reappeared at the door. He scowled at them before going to the stove and helping himself to a mug of coffee.

As he passed the table, he leaned a little closer to them. His expression was not friendly.

"You jetsam are costing us food and drink." His scowl deepened even further, if that was possible, then he straightened up and left.

The cook slid a bowl of bread soaked in milk in front of each of them. "This will be gentle enough for you to eat," he said. Looking behind him to make sure the First Mate had left, he added softly: "Don't mind him – he's just a good, old-fashioned bastard. I think his mother dropped him in a vat of vinegar when he was a baby. The captain... now, he's a good man."

They both finished the food before sitting and holding hands across the table. Salvation had come at last.

When he shook the cook's hand in gratitude, it felt warm and safe and solid, unlike the cruelly mercurial but unyielding sea surrounding them.

The man's grey eyes also held a warmth he thought he'd never see again during the bleak years that had just passed.

Then, despite his own exhaustion, he begged some hot water from the cook and washed his wife's swollen feet.

He had nearly finished when the First Mate re-appeared. "The Captain wants to see you," he grunted and led the way through the ship.

He was unused to all this metal around him and the way sounds reverberated against its surface sounded very alien to his ears. The engines were very loud but they sounded to him as if they were still losing their struggle against the sea.

The Captain's cabin seemed a lot cleaner than the other parts of the ship he'd seen. The man was smartly dressed and, standing before him, he suddenly became aware of how shabby his clothes were; stained, ragged and caked in swiftly drying salt.

The Captain asked his name and where he was from. The officer seemed satisfied with his answers and then asked why they'd been found drifting at sea, seemingly lost.

"We are pebbles. We go where we are tossed."

The Captain smiled grimly, obviously pleased by the comment. "And someone tossed you into the sea, eh?"

The man nodded. "Alright, well, we will drop you off at our next port of call."

Again, he nodded. "Please tell me, where are we headed?"

"Can you read?" asked the captain. When he nodded the uniformed man took his arm and led him out of the cabin. They passed along a corridor and up a set of stairs before crossing the gangway to the ship's bridge.

The helmsman spared a moment to look at the ragged figure being led in by the Captain.

Over the man's shoulder, the huge grey vista of the ocean stretched ahead outside the bridge windows. Even though he'd spent so long on the water, it seemed to be even more threatening constrained by the glass and metal frame. It felt to him like a huge beast on whose dark back they rode, ready to be shaken off and crushed like tiny, annoying fleas. His breathing became more difficult and he thought back to when he'd imagined his father's words about a salty death.

The Captain touched his elbow, bringing him back to the present. The two men went across to a large chart table at the rear of the bridge. Spread out upon it was a wide blue map with some darker parts around the edges.

The captain jabbed his finger at a point on one of the darker sections of the map. Leaning forward he read the name, but it meant nothing to him. He had no idea how far it was from his brother's home. But he knew that, at least, it wasn't in their own war-blighted country.

"It's the first time we'll have put in at that port. But our owners are hoping to open up a new trade route with the people there," said the captain.

He nodded. "I wish you well," he said, in a soft voice. Instead, he wished he had the luxury of contemplating growing trade, a better life, hope. Perhaps now he did have time for those things. There was a small kernel of hope in him now.

~

Later that day, the weather turned bad. Neither of them were used to such savagery. They huddled in fear in the kitchen, turning fearful eyes to the cook.

"Getting a bit rough, eh?" chuckled the cook, who was clearly not that disturbed by the ship lurching under his feet.

Great dark cliffs of water miles high pressed hard against the shuddering steel, crushing it between them. The ship groaned and creaked, as if it was ready to pop all its rivets and let the sea come flooding in, washing them clean of their lives.

He hugged his family to him, his frail arms encircling them to protect them as best he could. Every time the ship gave a shudder he felt a tiny piece being knocked off his heart. Though no longer sure if he believed in a God, or a being that could bring salvation of any sort, he prayed for the pounding noise to stop. His tears seemed an inadequate offering to any god that might be persuaded to watch over them.

Hours seemed to pass before the deck under them calmed. They held their breath, fearing the clamour might start up again but, after nearly an hour had passed, they felt able to let go of their fears.

As they enjoyed some strong tea brewed up by the cook, their nerves calmed gradually. Maybe life was good, after all.

~

He'd decided to go up on deck to get some air. He made his way to the bow and felt the wind and rain stinging his face. Just a day ago he would have hated the sensations, but now they made him feel truly alive.

He turned his back to the rain as it began to blow harder. He'd just decided to go back below when he happened to glance up at the bridge.

The First Mate stood gazing out through a pair of large binoculars. He followed the line of the man's gaze and tried to peer through the rain. He closed his eyes and wiped away the water, then opened them once again.

There, through the grey curtain of rain, was a harbour wall. He shielded his eyes and squinted; the wall seemed never-ending. The formidable, enormous slabs stared back at him with unyielding solidity. The tops of buildings could be seen beyond them, climbing up from the shore. But no entrance was in sight.

He squinted as best he could, unsure of whether he could be sure what he was seeing at this distance. It looked as if the wall was made of twisted figures, crawling in every direction over the wall, frozen and grey in their death throes. Their final agonies now trapped in stone forever.

It looked less like a harbour wall and more

like a fortress, meant to repel any intended invasion.

He stared up at the bridge, preparing to dash up there with news of what he'd seen, but it was obvious that the Captain and First Mate were arguing and pointing towards the harbour wall.

Suddenly the ship swung hard to port, seeking to turn away from its fatal course.

He heard the noise of the engines complaining loudly. Within seconds, there was a loud clanging sound from below decks and the engines cut out.

He headed back below decks as quickly as he could, fighting the wind and the swaying of the ship. Soaked and out of breath he stood in the doorway of the galley, gesticulating in the direction of the shore. The cook gazed at him and nodded.

Gathering them to him, the cook hurried the family up onto the deck. "This looks bad. We may have to launch the lifeboats," he muttered, before turning his eyes towards the shore and realising the foolishness of his words. No boat would stand a chance trapped between the sea and those rocks. Except they weren't rocks, he now saw. The entire shoreline was made of ships just like theirs, crushed and compacted, so that the rusty hulks made a landscape of mangled metal.

The tide grabbed the ship like a toy in a bathtub, flinging its bow towards the bizarre shore. An enormous shudder vibrated through the vessel as the keel scraped against a solid mass submerged just short of the shore.

The ship groaned in agony as something scraped against her belly, buckling her hull before breaking open the metal plates.

The cook ushered the man and his family towards the stern of the ship. "You stay here," he yelled through the spray and noise. "I'll be back..." Then he disappeared below decks.

Sailors' voices were raised in panic as the ship rose and fell like a bucking animal, trying to shake off its rider. Lifeboats crashed into the water as their davits were smashed against the jagged metal that supported the hellish wall.

There seemed to be no safety anywhere. His eyes scanned the shore as it raced towards them.

They clung to the taffrail as the ship bucked and twisted, the water lapping around their feet as the vessel continued its death throes.

"There... you see? We'll have to jump," he said, pointing.

She gazed at the place. The crumpled hull of an old steamer formed a shallow, angled shelf a few feet below them. It was broad and flat enough to stand on. As the ship lurched toward them she turned to him. "I'm scared!"

He held her to him. "I know. I know... but we will certainly die if we stay here."

Just then the vessel dashed itself against the dead ships and the angry sea gripped it and pulled it away. A few seconds later the ship's stern was heading back towards the jagged shore.

"Now. Now!" he urged her. Still clinging to the taffrail, she climbed the few feet as he held her waist. As the crumpled shore came closer, she bundled the child up and leapt for her life. She landed hard on one knee and yelped in pain. Looking up, she saw the wall towering above her, frozen limbs reaching out pleadingly as screaming mouths froze in a final scream. Hundreds of dead eyes gazed down at her.

Her attention was pulled away from the terrible sight when she heard her husband yell in relief at seeing them safe. Then the vessel was tugged away once again by the wild waters.

She stared as the ship took him from her, a soft moan beginning to rise at the back of her throat. He waved his arms wildly as the sea picked the ship up and took it a few yards farther away.

She feared he might be swept away from them for good. Moments later the pounding waters brought the ship back towards the shore and he climbed unsteadily on the rail, ready to jump.

At the moment he leapt into the air, the ship sank into a trough as the water raced away under it. He missed the rusted metal ledge and tumbled down before landing heavily on a wave-lashed rock below.

Screaming, she dashed to peer over the edge. She caught a glimpse of his face for just a moment, blood smeared and wearing a shocked expression, before the waves dragged him away and under.

Leaning over too far and reaching towards where he had been, the baby slipped from her grasp. It gave a small cry before plunging after its father into the angry waves. Tears blurred her vision and she saw the embroidered blanket the boy had been wrapped in bob to the surface once, before being snatched away forever. Her son was nowhere to be seen.

She made little desperate half-laughs at the back of her throat while her eyes scanned the unyielding water. Hysteria crept into her voice as it rose into a wail.

Her final scream of agony and loss was drowned by the crash of a huge wave as it swept her life away in the hungry froth of the white sea below.

Whenever she looks out of the window she has a view of a street emptied of houses. The holes where the shells fell are beginning to harbour a small forest of weeds and young trees. Occasionally a bird or small animal will venture through them, hoping for a scrap of food or some other advantage offered up freely by nature; they are seldom lucky. The woman sometimes cries while standing at the window but there is no-one now left to care or to wipe her tears. When the sun shines it merely irritates her, and she prays hard for winter.

The photograph in her hand shows a dark-haired boy and a man in his mid-30s. The man has light stubble and the boy has a brightness in his eyes that she remembers so well. The photograph is crumpled and creased badly along one edge where she struggled to free it from the grip of an angry woman. Yesterday, she saw the boy standing in the small scrap of garden that remains at the back of the house. His eyes were as bright as ever; quite different to when she saw him last. She quickly closed the curtains and turned away.

When it is cloudy and the sunshine is weak she stands in the tiny garden. Then she tries to remember it as it was, the ghost ground stretching away under her feet. She has never seen the boy while she's been in the garden; only from the window and only once, so far. The remnants of the flowers strain to appear beautiful, reaching for the sun. She hasn't seen a bee in the garden for well over three years. The abandoned woman stands in the abandoned garden waiting for the sunset. Then she will go inside and face the dreams.

The walls talk to her but it is hard for her to decide whether she is inside or outside of her dream. When she sleeps there are always images of the two of them, man and boy, walking towards her through cold morning mist. A crow accompanies them; it could be warning them or merely waiting for them to fall. Their slow footsteps are never numerous enough to reach her. The ground cannot support their weight. They fall and her heart falls with them. Then there is blackness, in the dark of the dream and in the hot, small room.

The alarm clock on the night table tells her another long day is here. Often she wishes she had no eyes so that she didn't have to look at its accusing face. The sweat of her dream still clings to her. When she stands in the shower and turns on the tap she counts it a small victory that there is water today. She washes quickly as the supply might end at any moment. Sometimes the water turns brown or red as if it contained excrement or blood. Then she presses herself against the cold tiles to avoid its touch.

It is only when her vision blurs and her cheeks grow warm that she realises that the face in the mirror is her own, crying. The face displeases her; she remembers as a child wishing that all the world's pretty things would disappear, so that she would be the prettiest thing left. The tear tracks cut through the filth on her cheeks. Despite endless washing, the layer of grime always remains. The air is thick with it, settling upon her skin constantly. She wonders if the water in the lake, just a short walk through the trees, will cleanse her.

The trees stand frozen in mid-dance, limbs twisted fancifully, straining towards gracefulness. Many are dead and have now been engulfed by the hungry moss, egged on by the dampness from the nearby lake. She clambers over those trunks that have fallen, recalling her lonely childhood forays into another wood, far from here. When she suddenly finds the water is at her feet, she stops and steps back, wanting to turn away. But she forces herself to approach it, staring down now into its black mirror. For the first time since she was a very young girl, the water frightens her.

The dark water reflects a night canvas back at her, swallowing the blue mid-morning sky and refusing to show it to her. Ripples bend the mirror, remoulding it from moment to moment, and playing hideous games with her face. Despite her unease at being next to the water, she finds the courage to reach out her hand and slap the surface, creating her own explosion, fragments of the day flying away. Eventually the water settles into a placid smoothness. In the depths of the mirror she sees a speck of white that may be the grudging reflection of a cloud.

Forgetting her intention in coming here, she kneels and peers down into the water. The white shape dances slowly as if caught in the secret nocturnal tides of the lake. It is no reflection of the sky but something that is wholly of this place that keeps things to itself. The object is moving towards her, falling upwards now, shaken loose from its submarine nest. A moment before it breaks the placid mirror, she realises it is a tiny bird's skull. It bobs before her, a reminder of her own death and her cherished dreams of flight from this land.

Lifting it carefully, it drips into her palm, like tears from the dead. She turns it over slowly, examining the empty orbits and the perfect curve of the beak. She remembers the boy holding out another bird's dry bones to her after his return from the park that once stood near the house. She had taken it from him and wiped the cobwebs from it. He'd told her of the birdhouse, hidden under the darkest tree at the edge of the park, and of the small avian skeleton secreted within. Dead too soon, she'd thought, like so many things here.

The empty eye sockets stare at her, sucking in her own gaze, negating her thoughts. She peers into the space behind them and feels how lovely it would feel to be so empty, so free of any painful duties of memory or feeling. The tiny cranium nestles in her palm, slowly leaking water onto her skin. The pool reflects the bone white accuser, reprimanding her silently for disturbing its rest and its lonely dreams of nothing. The sharpness of the small beak has been blunted by time and disuse. She thinks of how like this freshly liberated relic she is.

A chorus of birds seems to protest at the disturbance of their dead ancestor's remains, angry at her casual desecration of this avian relic. Then the woman notices that a man has emerged from the trees and realises it was a warning passed between beaks. Looking at him as he walks slowly towards her, she remembers the words of a childhood story: 'Suddenly a wolf came from out of the dark forest'. The man is shabbily dressed, and something covers part of his face. She catches her breath as she sees, just for a moment, the boy walking beside him.

The man clambers over fallen trees and splashes through the swampy shallows towards her. As he comes closer, she can see that what she thought was some sort of mask or an item of clothing over his face is really a scar. The sun catches the still livid areas of the old wound, giving him a frightening appearance. There is no boy with him, of course, and she thinks how stupid she was to have thought so. Soon the man is within a few feet of her. He stands, panting from his exertions, and breathes a woman's name; 'Teresa'.

She doesn't know what this man expects of her and turns away from him quickly. He repeats the woman's name and she wonders if he thinks she is that woman. She looks at the bird's cranium in her hands and, turning, holds it out to the man. Maybe she is making an offering to him, but maybe she hopes he can tell her something significant about it. He peers at it for a moment, uncertain of whether to take it from her, and then his damaged face creases in painful recognition. This time it is a boy's name he breathes.

There is something hidden behind the names which the man has spoken that plucks at her memory, like an insistent child at its parent's sleeve. She looks around at the shining flat lake, the surrounding trees, the white objects collected on the far shore, and wonders if she should even be here. But her memories stay stubbornly submerged beneath the surface; she wishes she could shake them free like she had done with the bird's skull. She feels the man's hand in hers, softer than she might have imagined it would be, and he says the woman's name once again.

The touch of his hand makes her feel wanted for the first time in a hundred years. All she can think of is the photograph of the man and the dark-haired boy, together. She looks up at the sky, reflecting blue, and tries to clear her mind. The sudden confusion of faces makes her want to weep. After a few moments, she forces herself to look at the man. The scar is horrific but, behind it, she sees at last the man in the photograph. His face is older now, much older than it should be, but it is him.

Although he is talking to her, she cannot follow the train of words. 'Wife' and 'home' mean nothing to her. She fights with her memories, struggling to get them to make sense, to stand in line as she's certain they should. She remembers him pulling at her arm, insisting that his way was the best; that it was best for all of them and that things would calm down again within a few months. It wasn't the fighting, or the soldiers, it was him. He had taken the boy away from her; this man had robbed her of her son.

He moves forward and takes her by the arm, expecting compliance. But now she hates the memory of her hands on him and refuses to go back to that place. She pulls away sharply and he shouts, forcing her footsteps to take her into the shallows of the lake, water welcoming her with its soft grip. He begins to follow her, huge boots breaking the water noisily. There is fear in her face, and she remembers what she is holding in her hand. Bringing it up, she drives it into his one smooth cheek, the tiny beak splintering in flesh.

The man yells in pain and advances further. She clambers onto a fallen tree at the water's edge in an effort to escape his anger. The tiny fragments of bone that she still holds drop from her hand and are forgotten. The blue sky frowns down. Memories of the boy's screams mingle with those of her own as the man stretches his hand out towards her. Her footing is unsure, and she slips backwards off her perch, avoiding his fingers by a whisper. He begins to clamber over the obstacle, losing his footing on the wet wood and falling hard.

She clambers out of the water, on all fours, and is ready to run. But all she can hear is the birds singing; no sounds of human anger, or pain, or renewed resentment. She dares to creep back to the tree and peers at where the man has fallen. His face is buried in wood, his head at an unnatural angle. Blood mingles with the dark water, darkening it further. She dares to reach out and touch him; the movement of his torso as his lungs fill and empty is missing. She climbs onto the tree. He is simply still.

'Water cannot stain' is her only thought as she watches his blood swirl slowly out. His absence has allowed her escape but only down a lonely path; no son and, now, no husband. She thinks of the house; it is the only thing waiting for her. After several minutes, her feet begin to carry her away from the lake. Gradually she makes her way back to the house. She stands in her room, praying that the rain will hold off and gazing out of the window at the scrap of ruined garden, hoping to see the boy appear once more.

As soon as he saw the room was empty, the young captain slipped his pistol back into its holster.

The colonel had fled, leaving many of his possessions behind. The sparsely decorated room with its low cot bed seemed far too modest for one of so high a rank. He smiled sourly to himself as he reflected on how sumptuously his own commanders lived.

On a desk pushed against one wall lay a pile of papers. He rifled through them quickly, looking for anything of value. There was nothing that they didn't already know, but underneath the pile lay a book.

Thinking it might be a code book, he picked it up. Headquarters would be pleased with anything that might help break the enemy's codes.

He opened it to the first few pages and groaned gruffly in disappointment. Words. Just words.

The cover had been torn off and there was no colophon or any publication information anywhere.

In fact, there was nothing to indicate it had been sold or distributed in any way. Yet it had obviously been professionally printed.

He began to read the first page. It was a journal of some sort, but clearly not the colonel's. The events detailed were not those of a soldier.

It had all happened a long time ago, judging by the language used by the author. Maybe it was from the last war. Or the one before. There had been so many to choose from.

He slipped the book into his pocket and joined his men to search the rest of the building.

~

That night he sat at his desk, illuminated by a single lamp as his pen scratched away at official papers and the hours slipped by. At last, he was able to close the folder.

From the next room came the restless sighs

of his wife, struggling to sleep because of the kicks inside her.

He slipped the book out of his pocket and placed it in front of him. The grubby white paper seemed to hold an indefinable promise. It was if the surface of the book was allowing the feeling to leak through his skin. He had no idea how many times the book had been read, but he had an unmistakable feeling that its previous readers had learned something valuable from it.

He began to read.

~

August 15th.

The guns fell silent a mere two days ago. A pall of smoke hangs over the city and I have no doubt that disease is already tightening its grip ever further on the unfortunate populace. There is ash on the wind this morning.

~

August 17th.

This scrap of land in a lonely stretch of cold sea is but a mile from the mainland.

They came in large, flat-bottomed boats that seemed to pay no heed to the week of unseasonably bad weather and rough water just passed. The capacious black barges are unlike anything we've seen before.

Jacob, my only neighbour on the island, says he has never known any boat to be able to land safely in the sort of weather that has filled the past days. And yet, the presence of these dozens of people seems to contradict his statement.

They have all arrived in various stages of undress or dishevelment. None of us have been able to get any of our strange visitors to speak. They do not seem to speak our language. Or any language at all, it seems.

Their faces hold no grace or threat but, from time to time, some betray an infinite sadness.

~

August 19th.

The newcomers have asked nothing of us. They want no food or water. None of them have sought shelter or asked us to allow them into our homes. What strange breed of people they are, I cannot guess. Yet they look like our fellow countrymen... our kin, even.

If only one of them would plead with us for some morsel or scrap of pity. A feeling of something inhumanly cold clings to them. I must be careful not to give my imaginings too much weight.

~

August 21st.

Jacob tells me that the sea-going barges in which our visitors arrived have vanished. Neither he nor his wife or servants saw or heard them depart, yet there is no wreckage upon the rocks or along the shoreline.

It is a mystery to Jacob who, being a farmer, is a purely practical man. And one who is used to the weather's strange and sudden changes. Yet nothing he has seen in nature explains the odd events to him, he claims.

I remember discovering that the name for this island in the old language meant 'knucklebone of God'. An overly poetic name for such a grey lump of land but I am perhaps beginning to see why people named it so.

~

Here, quietly, the dust had settled on his life. He was content with that... he would have been content with that, he meant, of course. But something about this unknown writer's words had raised a feeling of discontent in him.

It was foolish, he knew. He could simply stop reading this journal. It would be best to toss it in the rubbish bin or in the fire. But he simply could not.

He had re-discovered it only yesterday. There

in the back of the drawer, behind useless trinkets and mementoes, lay the unusual volume that he had found all those years ago and read for only a few days.

But in that short time, it had exerted an unusual influence on him. His memory of what it said was only vague, but he clearly remembered the sense of anticipation, almost foreboding, that he had felt when he had first begun to read it.

It had revealed no secrets to him in the past, but he had put it aside when the war and his private world had claimed his time. Colonels, wives and children all demand to be paid attention to.

Now he sought a redemption of sorts. Feeling resentment, he flipped the pages roughly between his fingers. Perhaps he did it in the hope that what he was looking for was hidden between the pages and would fall out if disturbed.

But he knew that whatever the book had to offer was buried within the words.

He remembered his Colonel once saying to him that one of the few benefits of a civil war was that everyone killed each other in the same language. And that this fact cut down on any unfortunate misunderstandings.

The man's sour humour felt devoid of any humanity at the time. But now language was so very important again, he realised. The cold-hearted old bastard might have had a point after all, in this time when words had once more become weapons. And lies were the new truth.

Fenced in on all sides, he dare not speak his mind.

Feeling a strange sort of despair, he determined to read on. Maybe he would find what he was seeking after all. He had nothing better to do with his time.

~

August 20th.

The girl who works on Jacob's farm called round with some eggs and milk this morning. She has a quick and persistent tongue and wears me out with her prattling.

She mentioned a passage in the Bible that said once Heaven was filled with the deserving dead, those who pass on will abide here on Earth.

I recall no such verses in the Good Book and suspect she may have misunderstood the original ones... if indeed they exist at all. I'm not even sure the girl can read.

~

August 22nd.

I have always found it difficult to enjoy the simple pleasures of life. Responsibility has weighed heavily on me and there were always too many duties to be performed to allow for much relaxation.

I had hoped my retirement here might afford me the opportunity to step away from that kind of life. This house, left to me by my uncle, was an ideal haven, it seemed.

Then death visited here to defy me, to mock my skills as a doctor. Try as hard as I might, I could not save my dear wife from his greedy grasp.

Then the war came...

Madness upon madness.

~

August 28th.

The barges are back, according to Jacob. No-one saw or heard them arrive but still they are on the shore.

The old orchard next to the house, which Jacob claims dates from before the island had any inhabitants, is crowded with figures. They stand as if dispossessed among the trees, not one of them bothering with the fruit offered so freely.

~

From the window of my bedroom I can just see the highest point on the island by craning my neck backwards.

Figures have begun to appear on the horizon. More each day, it seems to me.

There was a... monument at that place until recently. Now it is no longer visible, though it should have towered over the gathered figures by a metre or so.

Some referred to it as a cross, though I could never see a resemblance to any Christian symbol in its rough-hewn stones. Whatever it was, it was clearly very ancient.

~

August 30th.

They now fill every inch of this island, excepting the confines of this house. They have even taken over the use of Jacob's barn, I am told.

Yet they still have respect for my wife's grave, which lies behind the house. They stand, a field of figures, almost elbow to elbow, yet though they leave no room to pass by they have formed a cordon around the small scrap of earth where my Anna lies.

They have not encroached upon it at all; not one of them has set a foot upon it. For this, I am grateful.

~

I am beginning to feel isolated. Even during the lonely winters here, I never felt as I do now.

These people bring with them a loneliness I cannot understand. It seems to emanate from them. Yet how can so large a group of people all feel so alone?

~

August 31st.

They are at my door but I do not fear them. Not yet, at least.

When they move, on the rare occasions that they do, they remind me of the animals in Jacob's fields. That is the worst thing of all.

I find the weight of so much lost humanity to be a great strain upon my soul.

My wife believed in a God that I could not. Is this, perhaps, my punishment for such a lack of faith? Is He trying to force me to acknowledge that I have a soul... as if that would prove his existence to me?

~

Two cold stone memorials to dead sons and an insultingly minor post in the new Government. Bitter recompense for all his struggles. He has come to understand that loyalty is paid in a very poor coin.

During the war he'd been a noted tactician, often giving ground in order to secure eventual victory. Today his only strategy is surrender.

His wife and mistresses gone, his sons dead, his career in ashes. Sometimes he tries to convince himself that those he has lost merely failed to make the journey from the past to the present... that it was always their choice that they should not be here, never the result of decisions he made. Sometimes it helps. For a while.

"You sent our sons to their deaths!" she had said. He had heard his wife's words every day since.

~

September 1st.

At the back of the room, I felt sure I glimpsed the face of my daughter, Olivia. She was near to the door. Though the light was poor I felt sure it was she.

By the time I struggled through the throng, she was no longer there. I have not seen her since.

She left for the mainland late last year with her husband, so he could begin his book-keeping job. I do not know if they were caught in the city when the fighting started. I pray they are safe, even though I do not believe anyone is there to answer my pleas.

~

He closes the pages and slips the book back into the desk drawer, making sure to place it at the front, so it will not be misplaced again.

Propped up on the desk is a photograph of his sons. It was taken one summer, though they seem isolated from the sunlit landscape around them.

He'd treated them as men, though they were little more than boys. And how many dozens more were there?

Even through the twin lenses of passing time and the camera's gaze, the glint of growing hatred in his eldest son's eyes is very evident to him. If only they'd both known then...

Photographs are cruel things, he thinks. They tear you between the emotions captured in the image – whether it is happiness or not – and the sorrow piled upon it by the time that has passed since.

When he was young, he pushed his pride and vanity before him like a bow wave, ready to sweep everyone out of his path. Now he has arrived at a very dark shore.

~

September 3rd.

Even more people have arrived. Many are in uniform, though equally as many are not. Some bear wounds that are clearly unsurvivable. As a doctor, the conclusion is inevitable.

I am now convinced they suffer from a malady that neither myself nor any other physician can ever cure them of. Indeed, it is an affliction we know only too well and which has always mastered our efforts to defeat it.

If I am right, they are beyond the help of anyone mortal. Yet I have no idea at all why they have come here. Certainly it cannot be for me to cure them!

~

September 6th.

Through the window I can see the clouds darken over the black promontory visible from this part of the island. The lighthouse blinks out through the gathering gloom as the day continues to fade. The clouds do not look entirely natural. Maybe those in the city are beginning to burn their diseased dead. I dare not go out to check, even if they would let me.

It seems quite odd to reflect that maybe I am lucky not to be living in the city any longer. Though I also have a terrible sense of foreboding as to what this island is becoming. Perhaps a kind of refuge, yes. Or perhaps something much worse.

~

The mention of the dark promontory stirs something in his memory. He had been desperate at the time, falling back under heavy fire, but there was still an image in his mind from years ago. The promontory with a lighthouse. And an island in the distance.

He digs out some old maps and pores over them. He has a habit of remembering details of landscapes that were unimportant during the fighting. Often times they merely clutter up his mind, but today they might prove useful.

He unfolds another map and recognises the place at once. The dark island comes to the fore of his memory. And there it is, on the coloured paper sheet before him. Just a mile or so offshore, and barely 40 miles from where he now stands. He folds up the map and tucks it into his coat.

Then he picks up the book and slides it into his pocket next to the map. Only now can he understand the hope hidden behind the old doctor's words.

~

The driver steers carefully past the ruins of an old lighthouse and parks just above the narrow beach.

"Wait here," he tells the driver, who nods uninterestedly, then walks down the shingle to the thin margin of sand at the sea's edge.

Rain begins to dance on the calm surface of the water as he gazes across at the island. The shoreline seems to be devoid of life. Hearing a seabird's distant cry, he begins to search the skies. When it comes again he realises that it is only a small wheeze coming from his own chest, the legacy of a bullet from 20 years ago.

He digs one toe into the sand, which looks grey in the weak light from the cloud-heavy skies, scooping up a small amount to watch it fill swiftly with water.

He is convinced he is gazing at the island mentioned in the journal, though it looks much larger than it appeared on the map. He has the sudden, insane thought that perhaps it has grown larger with each conflict. And will continue to grow.

Raising his binoculars to his eyes, he squints hard. There is the farmhouse and the stand of trees nearby, the remains of the old orchard.

And everywhere – between the house and the trees, silhouetted against the sky, crowding along the shoreline – stand people. Waiting.

"My boys... are you there?" It is barely more than a whisper, though he wishes at once that he had shouted it, in defiance of the inevitable truth.

Returning his binoculars to their case, he once again drags the book from his pocket.

"For God's sake, be kind to me," he mutters to the nameless volume, knowing full well that the truth shows no mercy.

~

September 19th.

There is barely enough room left now to stand in one corner of this room to scribble in this journal. If another boat load arrives, we shall not survive.

A man stands mere inches from me. His face seems too large to me. I wonder if I am condemned to be fixed by his indifferent, empty gaze forever.

The dead are here, but where are the living? Am I the last one?

~

He closes the book and lets it drop from his fingers into the water lapping around his boots.

The book falls open on the blank pages at the back. Words begin to form on the empty whiteness but are washed away before reaching completion, black ink flooding across the page into the white foam.

The waves toy with the book for a moment before sucking it under, never to be read again.

He takes his first step into the sea.

Travelling Across the City in Autumn

We pride ourselves on being peace-loving creatures. Yet if you dare to peep at any newspaper or screen from behind your fingers it immediately becomes obvious that the one thing our species excels at is destroying each other.

And those who take part in any conflict inevitably carry the mental scars with them - many for the rest of their lives.

I began to wonder how a soldier would deal with those hidden wounds if they had to make a sudden, hard transition from killer to carer.

The chief protagonist isn't a particularly virtuous individual, despite his best efforts. He's just as deplorably fallible as the rest of us, in fact.

But at least he has a moment of clarity at the end of the story. I felt I owed him that.

Landfall

The inspiration for this story will be obvious to anyone who has followed the news over the last several years.

As a non-swimmer, being trapped at sea in a tiny boat that is likely to be swamped by the waves at any moment is one of the most awful things I can imagine. The courage and desperation of those willing to make such a journey makes me feel totally inadequate. And grateful, of course.

This is a particularly cruel story, I admit. I won't apologise for that because I believe it simply holds up a mirror to how the world actually works.

The Cobwebbed Bird House

This is by far the oldest story here. It started over a decade ago when an American poet friend of mine said "Let's write a book of haibun".

The expression on my face was no doubt the same as the one on your face right now.

Then he explained that a haibun was a Japanese literary form, which combined prose and haiku. Surprisingly, I agreed to the idea.

So I set out to write a story about the aftermath of war in paragraphs of 100 words, while he would write the haiku that linked the prose sections together.

We were going to write a short book of these ingenious things. But then life got in the way and he moved on to other things, so the only completed haibun went in the back of the metaphorical, digital drawer.

Which is where I found it several years ago. Reading it over, I thought it wasn't half bad. But those haiku would have to go.

The American biographer, critic and editor S T Joshi read it and was kind enough to publish the story in *Weird Fiction Review No. 8* in late 2017.

So that is why the numerologists among you will have spotted that each and every paragraph is exactly 100 words long.

I'd just like to stress that no poets were hurt in the writing of this story.

A War Unfought

Following the optimism of their youth, many people's lives are a long walk into loneliness and darkness. For a soldier, who has experienced the fear and heightened awareness of war, that contrast must make the end point of the journey all the more stark.

This thought collided with my admiration of Arnold Böcklin's eerie painting *Isle Of The Dead*. Beginning in 1880 he painted five versions, one of which belonged to Hitler ('belonged' in the sense that it was looted from its rightful owner, no doubt).

H R Giger's 1977 take on it, called *Hommage à Böcklin*, is even more unsettling.

A more hopeful version of the same destination is presented by guitarist Bill Nelson in the track 'Islands of the Dead' from Be-Bop Deluxe's brilliant 1978 album *Drastic Plastic*.

All of these things have lived in my head for some time so I decided to visit my own isle of the dead. This one is shared, at least briefly, with the bewildered living.

I'm fairly certain that this is the first time I've written about two main characters existing in different time periods. Maybe they're two sides of the same coin.

*Now available and forthcoming from
Black Shuck Shadows:*

Shadows 1 – The Spirits of Christmas

by Paul Kane

Shadows 2 – Tales of New Mexico

by Joseph D'Lacey

Shadows 3 – Unquiet Waters

by Thana Niveau

Shadows 4 – The Life Cycle

by Paul Kane

Shadows 5 – The Death of Boys

by Gary Fry

Shadows 6 – Broken on the Inside

by Phil Sloman

Shadows 7 – The Martledge Variations

by Simon Kurt Unsworth

Shadows 8 – Singing Back the Dark

by Simon Bestwick

Shadows 9 – Winter Freits
                                by Andrew David Barker

Shadows 10 – The Dead
                                        by Paul Kane

Shadows 11 – The Forest of Dead Children
                                        by Andrew Hook

Shadows 12 – At Home in the Shadows
                                        by Gary McMahon

Shadows 13 – Suffer Little Children
                                        by Penny Jones

Shadows 14 – Shadowcats
                                        by Anna Taborska

Shadows 15 – Flowers of War
                                        by Mark Howard Jones

blackshuckbooks.co.uk/shadows